LOVE THE ONE YOU'RE WITH

by

Robbie Moffat

PALM TREE PUBLISHING

PALM TREE PUBLISHING
Paisley, Scotland Pa1 1TJ

© Robbie Moffat 1999-2019

Film Rights © 2000 Palm Tree Universal
First published in digital form JULY 2014
First published in paperback JANUARY 2019

Typeset: Verdana 10.5pt

ISBN-10: 0 907282 26 1
ISBN-13: 978-0907282266

Chapter 1

It is Glasgow, 1999. Fast flowing city traffic on the move across the Kingston Bridge spanning the forlorn and slow moving River Clyde.

Exteriors of glass and steel, concrete and snarled slip-roads as traffic comes off the bridge and into the heart of the city.

The interior of the Trades House, Glassford Street, Glasgow. It is opulent from almost four hundred years of Protestant handshaking and deal making. It smells of old money in a modern world.

The hand of thirty year old business whiz-kid CHARLIE GRANT picks up a cheque for £500,000 made payable to Landtrust Securities. He places it to his lips and kisses it.

"Gentlemen, the future is real estate."

Charlie puts the cheque in his briefcase and quickly shakes the hands of two older men facing him.

On a table is a model of an enormous office tower.

Charlie puts on a pair of shades.

"Come Monday, you can start putting up your monument."

Detective Constable COLIN PATERSON is listening outside the office as his partner NEIL HOUSTON is screamed at by Deputy Chief Constable ROBERTSON who throws

Houston's warrant card into a drawer in his desk. Houston looks unrepentant.

"You are accused of bribing a witness in a murder case! Does that not bother you?"

"Someone stuck me in this shit. I want an investigation!"

Paterson, stuck to the wall on the other side of the door, with a look of guilt, mouths the word 'fuck'.

Outside the Trades House, a yellow Porsche is parked on double yellow lines. Charlie pulls a parking ticket from the windshield. He laughs and re-sticks it to the shield.

Charlie opens the trunk and swings his briefcase in.

He opens his briefcase and throws in his gold watch, his credit cards and his shades with the cheque, then snaps the case shut. He takes off his suit jacket and reaches for an old bomber jacket and puts it on.

He closes the trunk and smiles.

GINA MACKENZIE, twenty-two and streetwise, slips without a ticket into a cinema part way through the main feature. She takes a seat in the front row.

The sound of money going down kids' throats is spilling out of the 13th Note onto King Street.

Paterson is in the club in discussion with BINGO BROWN, a drug-dealing, moneylender, who is attended by his RUNNERS. Bingo is unhappy as he hands over an envelop of money to Paterson. Paterson smiles.

Gina sits watery-eyed sucking on a slush puppy watching the end of a movie as slushy as her shoes.

Charlie is in the Sub Club dancing drunkenly with an equally drunk CLUBBER GIRL wearing a long tight dress. Paterson pushes past him.

Gina leaves the cinema with a bag over her shoulder. It is obvious from the way she is dressed that she is poor and has nowhere to go.

Charlie is clinging on to the Clubber Girl trying to explain something over the music. The Clubber Girl can barely stand. Her dress is holding her up.
    "I live in London!"

Gina stops outside the night-club.
    "Hi, Peter. Got a cigarette?"
    PETER, a transvestite looks out of the shadows.
    "Hi, Gina darling. How was the picture?
    Gina stops to share a cigarette with Peter.
    Charlie, wildly drunk, comes staggering

out of the club with the Girl. Gina just avoids being knocked over by him.

"Watch it, you moron!"

The Clubber Girl and Charlie bundle each other into a taxi.

Peter and Gina exchanging knowing looks.

"Where are you going to stay tonight?"

"Lucy and I have made a skipper on some wasteland."

"Look out for the cops, luv. That bastard Paterson's on the streets this weekend."

Gina shakes her head as if she's heard it all before and walks off into the night.

It's morning and the Clubber Girls flat is strewn with empty Miller bottles. Outside is the sound of jamboree.

Charlie is on the Girl's sofa. His head is killing him. It is nearly eleven in the morning. He groans.

In the street, canary costumed dancers and peacock dressed paraders are assembling on Blythswood Square for the May Day Procession.

The Clubber Girl, wrapped in a terry bathrobe left over from a Carntyne jumble sale, is hungover, dishevelled and can't remember a thing.

"Whoever you are - you have to leave!"

Something in her urgency tells Charlie that it's all been a mistake. She gathers his clothes and forces him out of the sofa. Charlie is reluctant to go anywhere.

"What the hell have I done?"

Charlie dismisses the idea that she is upset because he hasn't screwed her. Was there a boyfriend? The Girl pushes him towards the door. She picks up her cat.

"You've overstayed your welcome."

She throws him out with the cat.

The door slams shut.

Out on a Glasgow street. George Street? Charlie is trying to get orientated. He has a bad hangover and everything is spinning. He sits on a wall and groans. He takes out his car keys from his pocket and stares at them.

Charlie returns to the spot where his car should be parked. He looks about. It is gone. He gropes in his jacket for his cell phone.

He dials 999. Pause.

"My Porsche has been stolen ..! This is an emergency. I'm stranded! Sorry ... no, it is not life threatening."

Charlie listens to a barrage of abuse. He holds the phone away from his ear.

"Look, I said I was sorry. Okay ..."

Pause.

"I parked it at Blythswood Square yesterday afternoon."

Expectant pause.

"Yes, that's the registration. Shit! In the city pound! Fuck!"

He kicks a street bin in fit of temper. He shakes his head as if it is all a bad dream and storms off.

It's twenty-five past noon. The Porsche is sitting behind an eight foot wire fence between two tow trucks. Charlie is in a sweat. He is arguing with the uniformed POUND CLERK who is behind a metal meshed high counter.

"You're behaving like a fucking policeman!"

"It's the law. No-one is allowed access to their vehicle until they've paid the fine."

Charlie empties out his pockets. There's nothing in them.

"Look, you imbecile. I haven't even got the price of a phone call. Do you think that I can just pull a hundred and five pounds out of my pocket by saying abracadabra?"

The Clerk ignores Charlie's ill-humour

"This is crap! What's the matter with you Glaswegians these days!"

The Clerk is starting to bring down the counter shutter.

"Hey, what the hell are you doing? "

"We close at twelve thirty on Saturdays. We won't be open again until eight a.m. Tuesday morning.

"Are you kidding me? What about Sunday and Monday?"

"Sunday we always close. Monday is a bank holiday."

The clerk pulls down the shutter and locks it in place. Charlie's face drains.

Outside the pound, Charlie is furious. He punches eleven numbers into his cell phone.

A plush apartment in London's Primrose Hill. CAROLINE ELLIS is being made love to by DAVID, a business associate, as she prepares a light lunch. She is opening the fridge door as the phone rings. She closes it.

There is a picture of Charlie and her stuck to the fridge door. She picks up the phone. Davis nibbles on her neck.

"Caroline speaking ....".

Charlie, with the cell phone to his ear, is thumped over the head with a short piece of wood by two JELLY ADDICTS.

He falls.

Caroline is listening into the phone. David has her dress around her waist and is massaging her buttocks with his eager hands. His fingers move lower. She gives David a resigned whimper.

" ..... wrong number?"

She replaces the phone and gives into David's wanderings.

The Addicts have dragged Charlie down an alley. They are rifling through his pockets. They take his phone, car keys, the last of his cash, and his bomber jacket.

They flee.

Charlie groans and tries to sit up. He is in his shirt sleeves. He feels the bump on the back of his head, and looks at his hand. There is no blood.

He gets to his feet. He staggers a little

"I don't believe this shit!"

Gina, wearing an old Bay City Rollers jacket, with her methadone ex-prostitute friend LUCY MURRAY, are 'ham and egging' their pitch in Royal Exchange Square. Lucy is selling the Issue, while Gina is across the way cross-legged begging with a cardboard sign stating that she is homeless.

Charlie appears in the square. He tries to stop PASSERS-BY.

"Could I borrow fifty pence to make a phone call?"

He is brushed aside. He sharpens his act

"Heh, how about fifty pence for a cup of tea?"

Gina sees Charlie. She leaves her pitch and gives Charlie a shove that sends him reeling.

"What the hell are you up to, pal? This is our pitch you're ham and egging on!"

Momentarily, Gina and Charlie's eyes meet.

"It's a free world." Turns away. "Fifty pee for a coffee, mister?

Gina is incensed by Charlie's attitude.

"You're asking for a kick in the balls, arsehole."

Charlie takes stock of her dyed ginger hair, spotty face, awful tartan jacket, black latex pants that are too short, and trainers that have been hand painted. He laughs.

"Look, darling, why don't you crawl back under the newspaper you came from. I'm having a bad day."

Charlie puts his hand to the back of his head and visibly wobbles. It is obvious he is in pain. He sinks to the pavement.

Lucy joins them. She looks at the gash on his head.

"He's been whacked."

Gina nods her head in realisation that she has been too quick to judge. She tries to help Charlie sit down on some steps

"My head is killing me."

"You need help, mister."

Charlie studies Lucy's bleached blonde hair, bloodshot eyes and chipped teeth.

"You two help me? All I need is fifty pence to call home."

"If you've been whacked, you should go to the cops."

"The cops? You're joking. I wouldn't be here if those bastards hadn't towed my car away."

Gina and Lucy exchange glances. They assess that he appears to be on the level. Gina reaches into her pocket and produces a phone card.

Charlie reaches out to take the card. Gina pulls it back.

"I'm coming with you. I don't trust anyone."

Caroline's telephone rings. The light lunch in the kitchen has been eaten. Caroline and David are naked and intertwined on the floor. The answer phone kicks in. It is Charlie's own voice.

"You have reached Chez Caroline's and Charles ...."

Charlie slams the receiver down in anger and pulls out the phone card from the payphone. Gina is genuinely concerned.

"Nobody home, eh? You look as though you could do with a meal."
Gina opens the door of the phone box. It creaks.

"Why don't you come with us and get something to eat?"

"Why should you do that?"

Charlie rubs his arms. Reduced to his Pierre Cardin shirt sleeves, he is feeling the cold. Gina is amused. She raises her eyebrows as if to say 'the choice is yours'.

"Well ... you look the sort of guy who's not used to missing meals. You'll freeze your balls off dressed like that."

Charlie shrugs his shoulders and follows her out of the phone-booth.

Colin Paterson and DREW GILMOUR, his new partner, are sitting in an unmarked police car across from the Soup Kitchen for the homeless and the unfortunate.

"They're all scum, Drew, every last dreg of them."

"They can't all be bad, Colin. Times are hard."

"Look, pal, maybe policing in Edinburgh is about being polite and sympathetic, but in Glasgow, you kick the shit out of the scum before you even ask them a question."

Gilmour is doubtful about Paterson's police methods. Paterson is eager to prove his point.

"Here's one of the scumbags now."

SNITCH, a duck and dive petty thief and junkie, approaches the car.

"Got any news for me, Snitch?"

"Nothing much, Mister Paterson. Everything's much the same except some new guy who's hanging out with some of the street bitches."

Paterson is curious.

"Is he a dealer?"

Snitch nods negatively. Paterson is looking for a motive but reveals his envy of people who might be enjoying themselves.

" Is he screwing them?"

"Don't tink so, Mister Paterson. Wan of the lassies is Lucy Murray. She split from Bingo Brown recently. Dae I get my Tenner Bag now?"

"Piss off before I get Gilmour here to do a warrant check on you."

Snitch backs away from the car quickly

and runs off.

Paterson takes a hip flask from his coat pocket.

"Fucking junkie."

He swigs some amber nectar from the flask then offers Gilmour a hit. Gilmour shakes his head and tries to hide his annoyance at Paterson's behaviour.

Paterson sneers at Gilmour. Come the end of the weekend shift, he'll tell Gilmour that he knows he is the chief constable's snitch.

The Soup Kitchen is in a large Greek Thompson church hall off St. Vincent Street. There are about fifteen tables seating seven or eight at a table. It is nearly one o'clock and everyone is waiting to be fed.

Gina, Lucy, Charlie are seated at a table with two pro's, DINA and BETTY (who has a black eye), and their two lookouts FOXY, an ex-con, and SILKY, a junkie. The eighth place is filled by STEAMER, an alcoholic.

Foxy sees that Charlie is depressed.

"You down on your luck, mate?"

Charlie nods.

"I'm just out of jail for breach of the peace."

Betty looks up with her black eye that Foxy has given her.

"And selling jellies ...."

"It was pinned on me, Betty. The bastards just wanted me off the streets."

"My arse ...."

Foxy glares at Betty as if to say 'Shut you're mouth, or I'm off'.

Gina diverts attention away from them

"How's life, Dina?"

"So so ... Foxy's looking out for me and Betty. Silky's too wasted most of the time."

Silky just smiles as if to confirm this is the truth.

Dina ignores him

"You selling the Issue now, Luce?"

"I've had it with the game. The streets are full of sicko's."

Everyone nods in agreement. The conversation is thin, but the concern is genuine.

"You still ham and egging, Gina?"

"Sometimes, Betty ...... We'll get the food."

Gina gets up and signals Lucy to follow her.

Gina and Lucy are piling some pompadoms on to a plate which are being handed to them by a soup-kitchen volunteer.

"Gina. Do you think he really is rich?"

"I don't know. He could be spinning us a line.

Gina and Lucy study Charlie from across the crowded soup-kitchen. Charlie looks lost. Lucy finds him attractive.

"I bet you he scrubs up nice."

"I was thinking the same thing."

"I'll toss you for him."

"He's not my type."

"He's not my type either. But neither was Bingo.

Lucy flips a coin. Gina calls.

"Heads ......"

The coin comes down heads. Lucy is disappointed.

"Shit .... best of three."

"No chance ... he's mine."

The eight-some around the table are finishing off their sponge custards. Charlie is scrapping his plate.

"That was great. Do you get meals like this everyday?"

Gina smiles.

"Most days."

Two swing doors are suddenly thrown open and FOUR VOLUNTEERS drag in some black plastic bags and begin emptying the contents on to the floor. Gina pushes back her chair.

"Come on, let's get you a jacket."

Gina is elbow to elbow with two MIDDLE AGED HAWKERS rummaging through the piles of clothes dumped on the floor. Charlie is behind her.

"God, those two are like hawkers."

"They are hawkers. They take this stuff and sell it down the Briggit market."

Gina pulls out a down jacket.

"Put this on!"

Charlie does as he's told. Gina continues to rummage and emerges with a sleeping bag.

"Here take this."

"No way! I'm not going to use it."

"Take it, you moron. I can sell that for a fiver."

Charlie does as he is told. He moans to Lucy.

"I bet I look like a retro."

"Yip ... but at least you'll be warm."

Gina is concluding her rummage. She has put some new clothes on herself. He thrusts a tie at him.

"Here a present. It's Calvin Klein."

Charlie meekly accepts the tie.

Paterson and Gilmour are still watching the entrance to the soup-kitchen from across the street. They are eating a Sarti's take-away. They see the girl's leaving with Charlie.

"There's Lucy Murray and her street partner. That's the new guy. What'd you think?

"Looks like a regular guy to me."

"They all look like regular guys until you do a check on them and find out that they have a record as long as a nigger's dick."

"You're a racist, Paterson. Maybe you should get off vice for awhile."

"And end up a pretty boy like you? I didn't ask for a new partner."

Paterson and Gilmour are suspicious of one another. Paterson is suddenly alert.

"Shit! I'll have to follow on foot. Take

the car and meet me at Buchanan and George."

Paterson leaves the car.

Gilmour's face reveals his frustration with Paterson.

Gina, Lucy and Charlie are walking down the West George Street Lane. At a distance, unnoticed, they are being tailed by Paterson.

Charlie, Gina and Lucy are standing by a pay phone. Charlie is pleading with Gina.

"Please, can I have you're phone card?

"So you can escape from us?"

Lucy rolls her eyes.

"While you two argue, I'm just going up the lane ..... "

Charlie and Gina are too engrossed to notice Lucy's departure.

"Okay, you can have fifty pence worth."

Charlie smiles, takes the card. They both squeeze into the phone booth.

Lucy is in the lane. He hands are shaking. She fumbles in her pockets and brings out a tenner bag of heroine. She feels her arm and a twinge crosses her face. She moistens her forefinger, sticks it into the 'h', then sticks her finger in her mouth.

The noise of the traffic is making it difficult for Charlie to speak on the phone. Gina stands listening.

"Look! You have no idea what I am

going through here. I've got the cheque in my briefcase .....

Gina can her Caroline on the other end of the phone.

"*Where the hell are you? The M25*?"

"I'm still in Glasgow."

"*Glasgow! You should have been here hours ago!*"

"Caroline! You don't understand."

"*All these years I've supported you, and now as soon as you have your own money, you don't want to come home.*"

"I love you, Caroline. Believe me. If I could be with you, I would." Turns to Gina. "The card's running out. Give me some money!"

Gina shakes her head. She is hurt by his actions.

"Give me more money!"

Gina resolutely refuses.

The phone goes dead. Charlie slams it down and reaches for the door.

"You blew it for me!"

He leaves Gina standing in the booth.

Lucy is licking the last of her tenner bag. Suddenly her hand is ripped from her mouth by Paterson.

"Up to your old tricks, love?"

"Get your hands off me, Colin!"

Paterson has begun to search her. He pulls out another tenner bag from her pocket.

Lucy freezes.

Paterson searches under her top and

pulls out some paper notes from her bra. He pockets the money. He pushes his hand down between her legs.

"Got anything hidden in there? What's the matter? You never used to complain.

Lucy remains unresponsive. She knows not to resist. She tries to hide her fear.

"Remember the first time I ran you in. You were so pleased to be let out you couldn't get enough of me.

Gina is at the bottom of the lane. She is searching for Lucy. She shouts out.

"Lucy!"

Paterson eases off.

"Everyone knows that junkie scum always ends up dead in the gutter. Stay away from the new boy or I'll tell Bingo you're screwing him."

Paterson propels Lucy on her way.

Further down the lane Lucy meets Gina who recognises Lucy's condition.

"Aw, girl! You've spent your money on that shit again! You promised me you'd stay on your programme."

She puts her arm around Lucy and whisks her away.

Gina and Lucy are back on their pitch in Royal Exchange Square. Gina is selling the Issue; Lucy is across the way sitting on some steps with Charlie. Lucy is spaced.

"Do you fancy her, then?"

"What sort of question is that?"

"Don't mess with my head. Just answer

me."

Lucy is nodding out. Charlie is concerned. He signals Gina over.

"What's wrong with her?"

"Haven't you seen a heroine addict before?"

Charlie is appalled. He recoils.

"Has she got aids?"

Gina gives Charlie a dirty look.

"Prop her up against the doorway. We'll just have to wait until she comes round.

Charlie is sitting on the sleeping bag with his head in his hands. Gina approaches and hands him a polystyrene cup of Matthew Algie coffee.

"I can't believe this is happening to me."

"Get real. Living on the streets is a way of life for thousands like us.

Lucy is awake. Gina screams at her.

"You should stick to your methadone. I'm sick and tired of being dragged down by people who can't get their lives together. That includes you!"

"I resent that!"

"Tough! Stop feeling sorry for yourself. What have you ever done for anyone but yourself? You probably live in some whitewashed villa in some tree lined street and think that you're doing well for yourself. But what about all the homeless kipping out in dumps and alleys like animals?"

"And that's all my fault? Look at her!

She's done that to herself!"

"Don't make me sick? You weren't abused by your father and sent to a foster home at the age of seven. What chance did she ever have when they sent her back to her alcoholic father at the age of eleven to be abused again."

"And that's my fault too?"

"Yes, it is your fault. The world is full of selfish uncaring pigs who don't give a flying about women like her.

"Wow, hold on a minute there. I give money to Oxfam and Unicef ...."

"To feed Africa! Great, what about this country. Don't you see the poverty! Of course you don't! You're head is up your arse!"

"Take a flying jump! People like you moan about inequality but meanwhile work the system to get everything they can for nothing."

"And you don't. I bet you cheat on your taxes and use every loophole in the law to get what you want?"

"I don't break the law."

"That's because people like you make them to suit yourself! We have to break the law to survive. So we steal, we beg, we recycle what we can to get by. We live off everything that no-one else wants."

"You're screwy! You're no better than a petty thief. You'll be an ugly bag of bones by the time you're thirty."

"At least I'm not already ugly like you. You hate everybody who's not like you.

Maybe that's why nobody loves you."

Gina helps Lucy to her feet. Gina pulls the sleeping bag from under Charlie.

"You can go to hell!"

Gina and Lucy disappear through the Royal Exchange archway. Charlie is glad to see the back of them.

Gilmour is sitting in the unmarked car at the junction of Buchanan and West Nile. He is reading Irvine Welsh's *Filth*. Paterson gets in the front of the car. Snitch gets in the back.

Gilmour is pissed off with Paterson.

"Where the hell have you been?"

"Shopping. Drive round to Queen Street!"

Gilmour gives a look that demands an explanation.

"Just do as your told, Gilmour, and we'll get on just fine."

Charlie is stopping passers-by outside the Modern Art Museum.

"Hi. My name's Charles Grant and I need some money to ...."

A Pedestrian gives him a look of disgust and brushes past.

Charlie tries to stop a Woman going past.

"Hi. My name is Charles and I need some money to get a bed for the night."

The Woman ignores him. Charlie pursues her.

"Look ... I'm hard up ....!"

The unmarked police car pulls up across the street. Paterson rolls down the window.

"There's Pretty Boy."

Gilmour cranes his neck to look.

"He looks harmless to me."

"Remember your training, Gilmour?

"What's that?"

"Your job as a police officer is to prevent crime before it happens."

Paterson throws open the back door and motions Snitch to get out.

Charlie is failing to get any passers-by to help him. They all brush past. He turns to look in a tailor's shop window displaying suited mannequins. He sees his own reflection. He realises he is no longer the guy he thinks he is.

Snitch creeps up on him.

"Heh, man ... wannt tae half a bag wi' me?"

"Are you talking to me?"

"Sure, man. A've only 'nough fur a couple a' jellies. But if we split in, we could score a ten bag."

"What are you talking about?"

"Aitch, man. The Busies wannt tae know if yi' jag it!"

Snitch throws his head in the direction of the unmarked car.

Charlie looks blankly at Snitch. He is trying hard to understand him.

"They're making me dae this, man. If a

wis you, a'd blow. That cop's a mean fucker. He'll stitch you up."

"What are you talking about?"

"In the cor, man."

Charlie looks across the street to the unmarked car, but it means nothing to him.

"Shake yer heed to show yi' don't wannt tae score, an' a'll blaw."

Charlie shakes his head. Snitch smiles and staggers off.

Charlie stares after Snitch then loses interest.

Snitch approaches the dark blue Vectra and gets in.

"Dae I get my tenner bag, noo?"

Paterson grabs Snitch by the throat and pushes him away.

"Fuck off, scumbag!"

It is late afternoon and Argyle Street is busy with shoppers. A minute's walk away in King Street, BINGO BROWN is operating from a street bench with a cell phone. Bingo is surrounded by TOMMY, his right-hand man, and his runners, GERRY and ANN-MARIE, the same pair of addicts who had whacked Charlie outside the city pound.

Also on the bench, with Bingo, is Snitch who is unhappy with how he is being treated.

"I tell you, Bingo, that Paterson has flipped. They've suspended his regular partner and stuck him with a dodo."

"The fucker! I already gave him a cut of the Giro's and the Monday Books!"

"Paterson uses me like bog roll. I'm sick of wiping his arse."

"Okay, Snitch. You know I look after my boys. Get Tommy to count you some jellies."

"Thanks, Bingo."

Snitch moves away to speak with Tommy.

Bingo beckons Gerry and Ann-Marie..

"Put the word out that Paterson is on the shake and that no-one is to carry more than the score they're delivering. And warn the girls. I know Paterson's game, if he can't bleed us, he'll do some tart over for her quick tenners."

Charlie, sick of panhandling, is down by the riverside contemplating his life. He is sitting on the embankment wall behind the boarded up restaurant that was the haunt of the Bisto Boys during the city's year of Culture a decade earlier.

From the Suspension Bridge above him, Paterson and Gilmour are staring at Charlie contemplating his scuffed up Italian shoes.

Charlie is angry for allowing himself to become stranded in Glasgow.

"My shoes are fucking ruined."

In a vain attempt to restore his dignity, he tries to polish them with the sleeve of his soup-kitchen coat.

Paterson and Gilmour are standing over him.

Charlie looks up. Paterson is waving his warrant card.

"Get up, scumbag."

"I haven't done anything wrong."

"What's your name?"

"Charles Stuart Grant."

"Address?"

"23 Primrose Lane, London."

Gilmour moves off a little way and starts talking into his handset.

"Is that a hostel?"

Charlie draws a face that says 'Fuck off, you cheeky bastard'. Paterson uses Charlie's non-co-operative attitude to his advantage.

"Turn out your pockets!"

Charlie suddenly finds himself being frisked by Paterson.

Control has replied to Gilmour's information. He rejoins them.

"The only thing outstanding on a Charles Grant is an unpaid pound ticket on a Porsche."

Paterson and Gilmour both laugh.

"It's my car!... Look, I know I should have gone to the police as soon as I found myself penniless, but I was pissed off. Okay? Now, I realise that you are the only ones that can really help me."

"Shut up, arsehole!"

Paterson slaps Charlie across the face. Gilmour is visibly distressed by Paterson's behaviour.

Charlie remains controlled.

"Are you threatening me?"

"Hear that, Gilmour, a homeless scumbag who hasn't learned to smile through his teeth."

Paterson hits Charlie again, this time with the back of his hand. Charlie reels from the blow. Paterson wipes his hand, sneers and whispers in Charlie's ear so that Gilmour cannot hear.

"We like to send scum like you in a dumpster to the city incinerator."

Paterson turns and walks away.

Gilmour pauses to give Charlie a look of 'What was that all about?', then follows after Paterson.

Charlie feels his jaw to make sure it is not broken.

Chapter 2

It is evening and the light is dropping off in the west. Although it is the first night of May, there is a chill in the air and Charlie is trudging the streets to stay warm.

The street lights come on. Charlie slumps on a park bench in George Square and dozes off.

It is now nightfall. The bright City Chamber lights cast a warm glow on the eastern side of the square. Charlie is still asleep on a bench. On the bench next to him is WILLIE BOY, a wide-eyed Highlander from Inverness who has wandered the world.

Charlie wakes. Willie-Boy thrusts a Virgin Cola bottle at him.

"Want a wee drink?"

Charlie eyes Willie-Boy, then the bottle.

"Thanks. I'm parched."

Charlie takes a swig from the bottle. He almost chokes and spits the liquid out.

"What the hell is this? Vodka???"

"It's in case the busies stop me."

Pause.

"Are going over to the soup kitchen?"

"No, I can't be bothered walking all the way back there."

"Don't be daft, man. It's right behind you."

A line of NIGHT SOUPERS are queuing by

the statue of Robert Burns. Charlie and Steamer are standing in line waiting to be fed.

"I might have known that scrounger would be here."

Charlie swings around to see Gina.

Gina has changed her clothes, and is clean.

Gina draws his eye to Lucy talking to some Night Soupers.

"Just thought we'd pop out for some supper. How about you?"

"I'm on a diet. Thought I'd let lunch digest before eating again."

They both laugh nervously.

"I looked for you earlier ...."

"I didn't know you cared?"

"I just wondered if you'd managed to get sorted out. Obviously not ...."

"No. All I got was a bruise on my jaw to match the bump on my head."

Gina is not sure what he's talking about.

"Look, I'm sorry about earlier."

"Forget it. I'm beginning to understand why you might have a grudge against the world."

"I don't have a grudge!"

"See! That prove's it. You can't have a normal conversation with people without blowing your top."

"Have you ever thought for a moment that it might be you? That you're the one with the grudge at having to stand in line with a bunch of ...?"

"Losers! You've got it right there, sweetheart."

"Welcome to the club!"

"What do you mean by that?"

"So you're here by choice are you?"

"Everyone's here by choice, sister. No-one needs to be standing in this line in this day and age. This isn't the time of Burns."

"So why are we all here? Eh? Have you got an answer for that?"

Charlie and Gina receive a cold ham roll from a VOLUNTEER.

"Look, I'm too bloody hunger to give answers to a kid that left school at sixteen."

"So your university education has saved you from being riff raff?"

"It certainly has. I've made something of my life.

"How???"

"I've got a nice house, a car, a good job, and more money than I know what to do with."

Everyone around Charlie laughs.

"What's so funny? Do you think I'm going to spend the rest of my life standing in a line with you down-and-outs?"

Willie-Boy, who is talking with Lucy, is angered.

"You won't have any legs to stand in line with us if you keep talking like that, you numpty."

Gina holds up her hand to Willie-Boy to

tell him to go easy.

"We're all in this together. Nobody wants to be here. So just eat your food, and drink your tea. Okay?"

"Sorry .... I didn't mean to upset anyone.

"It's okay. It's your first day. They understand better than you think."

"That's right, man. Forget it." Wiilie-Boy is drunk. "Has he got a place for the night?"

Gina shakes her head.

"Heh, man ... I can get you into the spike for the night. It's got clean beds and you'll get a breakfast in the morning."

Gina reassures Charlie that the offer is genuine.

"You'll have to make up a story. They don't like rich types where we're going."

Everyone laughs except Charlie.

Lucy gives Willie-Boy a kiss and rises. It is obvious that Willie-Boy is struck on Lucy. Gina takes Lucy by the arm.

"We're off. Take care of him, Willie-Boy."

Charlie stares at Gina with pleading eyes. She senses that he would rather be with her than Willie-Boy.

"I'll maybe see you tomorrow."

Gina and Lucy depart. Willie-Boy starts to shift. Charlie follows.

Willie-Boy halts Charlie under the gaze of one of the guarding lion's of the white granite cenotaph.

"When they ask you where you last lived, you say 'I was evicted from my girlfriend's yesterday.'

Charlie repeats. "I was evicted from my girlfriend's yesterday."

"Then they'll ask if anyone can vouch for you. They have to have a Glasgow address."

"My parents live in the Southside."

"Are you kidding me? You're from Glasgow?"

Charlie nods.

"Christ sake!"

"I've been away fifteen years."

"Don't tell them that. Give the address but say 'they've disowned me and I don't want them contacted'. Say it."

Charlie tries to recall his lost Glaswegian accent.

"Ma parents have disown'd me an' a don't wannt them contact'it."

"Then you say 'I've arranged with the social to pick up my giro at Minerva Street on Monday.'"

"A've arrang'it tae pick up ma giro at Minerva Street oan Monday."

"Good, I think you've got a chance."

Willie-Boy takes some of the contents of his cola bottle and slaps it on Charlie's face like cologne.

He makes Charlie take a swig, then takes a swig himself.

"Swagger a little bit ..."

Charlie pretends to act as if drunk, and Willie-Boy laughs uproariously.

"That's it. Good. I think we're ready to face the management."

The reception area of a bleak men's hostel in Duke Street. The HOSTEL MANAGER has the appearance of a social worker. He is listening to Charlie's story. Willie-Boy is giving Charlie a nudge.

"I've arranged to pick my giro up at Minerva Street on Monday."

The Hostel Manager eyes him queerly.

"Monday's a bank holiday?"

Willie-Boy intercedes.

"He means Tuesday."

"All right, fill in these forms. You can share a room with this gentleman. You can stay until we can get your housing claim sorted out on Tuesday.

Willie-Boy gives Charlie a wink, and with a little push from him, they climb the stairs.

Charlie is shown his bed which is one of many in the room. He is shocked at the conditions.

"That's you're bed there."

Willie-Boy sniffs the air.

"Who's pissed in here?"

A coarse hacked-off voice comes floating through the gloom.

"Fuck off!"

Willie-Boy shrugs his shoulders and sits on his bed. Many of the beds already contain sleepers. Charlie sits down on the edge of his bed wondering if anyone is going to take a fancy to his clothes.

"The beds are good ... but that's about all you can say about this place."

A twenty-year boy from Yorkshire called SMOKEY is lounging on a bed nearby. He is rolling a joint and joins the conversation.

"You've come to a good house, and yer don't know it."

Two beds along, a twenty-eight year old dosser from Falkirk called STEAMER, chips in

"If I hadn't been drunk last night and got chucked out of my regular place I wouldn't be here now."

The course voice from the gloom rasps out again.

"Give over will ye? When are you chancers goan' to sleep. Ah've work in the morning. Fuck me if ye havnae robbed me of my kip. Take care ah don't set about ye's."

Willie-Boy is taking nonsense from nobody.

"Fuck off, you old alkie!"

He raises his eyebrows to Charlie and smiles as if to say not to worry

"Here ... you want a blow?"

Smokey hands Willie-Boy a joint.

"Who's your new pal, Willie-Boy?"

Willie is caught in the middle of a draw. He remembers Charlie.

"What did you say your name was?"

"Charlie ...."

"Aye, right. I'm Willie-Boy, this is

Smokey, and that's Steamer."

Steamer plonks himself down on Charlie's bed.

"Are you doing it with that Gina lassie?"

Willie-Boy is angered by Steamer's comment.

"Shut up, Steamer. Everybody knows Gina's been messed up since her old man topped himself."

Smokey is surprised. "I didn't know that, man."

"He was a dealer, man. Swears she knew nothing about what was going down. She came home found his head in lavvy. O.D'd on smack. Lost the flat, everything."

Charlie is shocked.

"Christ ...."

"It gets worse, man. She was pregnant. Council gives her a new flat. A month to go she loses the baby. The council chucked her out on the street."

"Why?"

"She wasn't pregnant any more. End of their responsibility. If the kid had lived she'd still be in the flat.

Smokey lets out a pissed-off hiss.

"The system's fucked, man."

Everyone nods. All of them have had their lives flushed by the system.

Some time later, and Steamer is fast asleep on his own bed. Willie-Boy and Charlie are sitting on the floor passing a joint. Smokey is stretched across

Charlie's bed.

"I was married ten years, then my wife left me. The house was in her name, so I was forced out by the council."

Willie takes a long draw on the blow.

"I loved her, man. I hit the skids. I need to cut down on the eccies to get my head straight."

Steamer nudges Charlie.

"He's in debt to Bingo Brown."

"It's true, man. He has a lean on my giro. On top of that, I'm doing a thing with that Lucy lassie, and Bingo's in love with her."

Smokey has heard it all before. He's more interested in Charlie.

"What about you, man? You got a wife?"

"Naa....."

"A girlfriend?"

"I suppose you could call her that. It's more like a business arrangement."

Willie-Boy detects Charlie's ambivalence.

"Do you love her, man?"

"I thought I did ....."

"Where does she live?"

"London."

A look of alertness comes into Smokey's stoned eyes.

"You from London, man? I sold the Issue in Piccadilly."

Charlie smiles weakly. Willie-Boy let's out about Charlie's origins.

"His parents live in Glasgow."

"Glasgow? Why aren't you staying with them instead of this doss house?"

Charlie half smiles. "It's a long story."

"Shut up, will ye!" the voice cackles. "If I come after yer bodies, yi'll know it, no mistake aboot it."

No more is said. Charlie is left holding the joint as Smokey returns to his own bed. Willie-Boy turns over on his side.

Charlie carefully takes his Italian shoes off and places them under his bed. He lies on his back and quietly smokes the joint. He reflects on the day he has had.

Steamer is snoring.

Charlie stubs out the butt of the joint on the floor. He looks up and catches Willie-Boy looking at him.

"That Gina, man, reminds me of my wife. She's different from the rest of us. You should be nicer to her next time you meet."

Willie-Boy turns over.

Charlie thinks about what he has said, then turns away.

It's morning. In the hostel wash room, Charlie is stripped to the waist. Smokey and Steamer are washing themselves. Willie-Boy is shaving. Everyone has their own soap and towel.

"Can I borrow your razor?"

"You might have aids, man."

Charlie recalls his remark about Lucy.

"Come on, man. Do I look like a junkie?"

Willie-Boy looks Charlie up and down then passes Charlie the razor. Smokey is curious.

"Is it true, man, that you've got a Porsche?"

"That's right."

Willie-Boy laughs.

"What's so funny? I'm on the level. My car's in the pound for the weekend, and all my credit cards are in the boot."

Willie-Boy smirks. He thinks it's a joke.

"Including your VISA card?"

"Including my American Express, Mastercard, and Visa cards."

Willie laughs again. He's not sure whether Charlie is on the level or not.

Charlie is the last to return from the wash room to the main dormitory. He is alone, everyone else has cleared out. He suddenly notices that his clothes are gone. In their place are some old clothes - a grey polo-shirt and a tartan padded jacket.

In hope, he reaches under the bed for his Italian shoes. He pulls out a pair of trainers.

"Fucking bastards."

He slumps on the bed and sits motionless trying to contemplate where he has gone wrong in life.

Gina is waiting outside the hostel. She is clean and sensibly dressed.

Charlie comes out of the hostel wearing

the tartan jacket and trainers. He sees Gina waiting for him. He is so relieved to see a familiar face, he hugs her.

"You smell nice."

Gina is restrained. She frowns at his clothes.

"Sleep well?"

"I'm never going back in there. I'd rather sleep under a tree."

"You're starting to talk like one of the boys."

Charlie laughs at himself.

"Did you get your breakfast?"

"No ... I slept in."

"Well, seeing it's Sunday. I'll treat you.

It is a poor part of the city centre down near the river. There are still very few people about. Gina and Charlie are walking and talking idly.

"You amaze me. Every time I see you you're dressed differently."

"When you're homeless, you don't have to wear a uniform. You can be whoever you imagine yourself to be. Besides, living on the streets you go through clothes like normal people go through money."

"I'm glad I'm normal?"

Gina looks at his trainers and laughs.

"I think you used to be, but not any more."

"My shoes cost an awful lot of money."

"People get too sentimental about what they buy. They have wardrobes full of stuff they don't care about. Eventually it'll end up in some charity shop, then it'll come down to people like me to wear."

It is a small city centre cafe. Gina and Charlie have finished their breakfast and are sitting sipping coffee.

"I was adopted at birth but ended up in foster care. My foster parents gave me everything I could have wanted. Then at fifteen I fell in love with a boy called Rab ... married him as soon as I could. We got a flat, and as long as Rab was happy everything was fine. Then one day when he was at work his best mate Kenny raped me. Rab beat me up.

Gina can't look Charlie in the eye. Charlie reassures her by pressing her hand into his.

"When I came out of hospital, my foster parents took me back. I got a job ... got a divorce. Then I met Billy. Then I lost the baby. Then I took off. And now, here I am ... twenty two and nothing."

"That's not what I see ..?"

"Thanks ...."

"Look, will you let me show you something?"

Gina nods.

In the heart of city between George and Argyll Street there is a wasteland of open ground surrounded by buildings. Charlie and Gina are standing on the wasteland and Charlie is expansively waving his arms around.

"I sold this land on Friday to some developers for half a million pounds."

"What are they going to do with it?"

"They are going to put up the highest office block in Europe."

"You're kidding me?"

"Nope, it's going to be sixty stories high. From the top you are going to be able to see right across Scotland - from the Atlantic to the North Sea."

"That's crazy."

"What's crazy about it?"

"It's just ridiculous."

"Why?"

"We're a tiny little country. Why do we need the biggest office block in Europe?"

"Just because we're tiny, doesn't mean to say we can't think big?"

The logic of this sinks in with Gina.

"But bigger doesn't mean it's better?"

Charlie thinks it over, and agrees.

"True. Look, I think I need another coffee before you convince me that small is beautiful."

They both laugh. Charlie takes Gina by at the arm and leads her off the wasteland.

Paterson is with his daughter Charlotte in a Southside park. She is a well-dressed ten year old who lacks nothing in life. She is riding her new bike bought by her dad.

"You like it, Charlotte?"

"I love it, dad. It's the one I wanted."

Charlotte gives Paterson a hug.

"Why do I only get to see you on Sundays before church, dad?"

"Your Mummy has a bad temper."

"Will I see you in the summer holidays? Mummy wants me to go to Gran's in America for the whole summer."

"You'll love America. It's a great place."

"Why can't I live with you, dad?"

"It's my job, honey. It takes up all my time."

"Do you lock people up all the time?"

"Only bad people."

Paterson stuffs a ten pound note into Charlotte's coat pocket.

"There are a lot a bad people in the world, Charlotte. They try to give children drugs to make them bad like themselves. It's my job to make sure that they never come anywhere near children like you."

Paterson gives Charlotte a kiss. She throws her arms around his neck.

"I love you, Dad."

Paterson hugs her tight for what seems like an eternity. They are both broken by the separation that keeps them apart.

"Come on. I'll give you a race back to the house."

Paterson starts running. Charlotte chases him on her bike.

Gilmour is standing on a golf green talking to Deputy Chief Constable Robertson who is practising his putting.

"So what have you found out,

Andrew?"

"He's on the take, sir. I haven't got anything definite yet, he's a bit of a loner when it comes to street work."

"In what way?"

"He just takes off and leaves me sitting in the car for most of the shift. I think he's skimming the dealers and the tarts in return for turning a blind eye."

"If there's one thing I hate, it's a bent cop."

Roberston continues to putt.

"Statistics, Andrew, arrests and prosecutions, always show up a copper who's on the take. In the last two years, Paterson's sheet hardly shows anyone who's gone down for more than six months. Outstanding warrants, itinerants, breaches of the peace, prostitutes ... not one major dealer, thief, or known heavy."

"Paterson must be taking his ex-partner's drink as well as his own share."

"Corruption is endemic, Andrew. Although we have Houston on suspension, we can't prove a thing. We need to catch Paterson at it and then they'll both go down for corruption as well as bribery."

Robertson plays a ball towards the hole. He runs it past the flag by ten feet. He start towards the flag, beckoning Gilmour to follow.

"Does anyone in the section suspect you're from the Criminal Investigation Branch?"

"Someone's tipped him off. He's cagey with me. It's not going to be easy, but if he's rattled enough, he'll make a mistake."

"Nail him, Andrew! I don't want it getting out in the press that my police force is just as corrupt as the councillors at the City Chambers."

"Do you want me to report to you at the end of the shift?"

"Leave it to Tuesday morning, Andrew. Tomorrow's a bank holiday. Nothing much is going to happen in forty eight hours."

Chapter 3

Gina and Charlie are strolling on Glasgow Green.

"How would you like to spend the rest of the day with me?"

"What have you got in mind?"

"I though we'd maybe take a train out to Loch Lomond and go for a swim."

"A swim! At this time of year?"

"Sure. It's May."

"I haven't any money for the fare?"

"That's not a problem."

"You're determined aren't you?"

"I just know what I want. But first, I'll need to let Lucy know where I'm going. Come on."

Willie-Boy, Smokey and Steamer are staring through the wire mesh of the car pound.   Steamer points to a yellow car.

"There it is!"

Smokey is dismissive.

"That's a Skoda, numskull."

Willie-Boy smiles, and points with the crow bar in his hand.

"That's a Porsche Nine-Eleven."

The eyes of the other two light up at seeing Charlie's car wedged between two tow trucks. Steamer is amazed.

"He was telling the truth."

Willie-Boy has climbed the fence and is inside the compound. He creeps up on the Porsche and is full of admiration for

Charlie's style.

"Nice car, Charlie man."

Willie-Boy tries to find a place with the crow bar to jemmy open the boot. He sees a reflection in the polished paint work. He looks up.

Smokey has got his trouser leg caught on the barbed wire at the top of the pound fence and is dangling upside down.

"I'm stuck, man. Aw, man, help me. I'm too wasted."

Steamer is trying to help Smokey down. He is alarmed that they are going to be caught by the Pound Clerk.

"For fuck sake, man. Shut up!"

Meanwhile, Willie-Boy is transfixed. A German Shepherd is staring at him from the end of a leash held by the POUND GUARD.

Willie-Boy drops the crowbar and runs. He scrambles over the barbed-wire. The dog is snarling and jumping at his heels. Steamer pulls Willie-Boy over and they both make their escape.

Smokey is left dangling on the wire.

"Heh, man! Willie-Boy! Steamer! Heh!"

The Pound Guard grabs Smokey off the wire, wrestles him to the ground and forces his arm up his back.

Smokey cries out. He knows for certain that he's going straight to jail.

Outside Pitt Street Police Station, Paterson and Gilmour are walking towards their parked unmarked car.

"I've been checking up on you, Drew."

"Oh, yeah ....."

"A pal in Edinburgh tells me you were with the Met before transferring back up north. That's why you've got that ponsey accent."

"Make you feel inferior, does it Colin? Frightened because I read books?"

"That's what it must be, partner - that Presbyterian bible you read every night before you go to bed?"

There is the sound of the St George Tron Bells. Paterson looks up.

"Sundays ... I love them. Hear the church bells? It makes me come over all righteous."

Gilmour gives Paterson a 'fuck-you" smile and gets in the car. Paterson laughs.

Gina and Charlie meet Dina standing on a corner in Blackfriars Street.

"Have you seen Lucy?"

"She's up the lane with a trick. I'm looking out for her. Silkies's too wasted."

Gina is not pleased.

A YOUNG MAN comes out of the lane. Gina and Charlie look the other way. Lucy follows shortly after, smoothing down her clothes.

"Cheapskate. He wanted it for a tenner."

Charlie is uneasy with the conversation.

"You should give it up, Luce."

"And get a job pulling pints? That'll be

the day."

Unnoticed, while they are talking, the unmarked police car pulls up. Paterson and Gilmour get out.

Lucy sees Paterson and is alarmed.

"Keep that pervert away from me."

"Well, we've got a right little chapel gathering here. A tart, a thief, and a scumbag."

"Piss off, Colin. We're doing nothing."
Paterson points out Gina to Gilmour.

"Grab Ginger ...."

Gilmour takes hold of Gina and starts to hustle her off. Paterson grabs Lucy by the wrist and jerks her towards the car. Charlie intercedes.

"Hold it! That's police brutality."

"I thought you were gone, scum. Shut it, or I'll call you in."

Charlie knows that he hasn't a chance of taking on the law. He backs off. Paterson throws Lucy against the far side of the car. She is struggling. She lets out a cry of pain.

Gilmour puts Gina into the car.

"What the hell are they being arrested for?"

"Soliciting in broad daylight. It's Sunday. They should be in confessional."

Paterson pushes Lucy into the back of the car with Gina and closes the door. Charlie goes up to the car and speaks to Gilmour.

"This is wrongful arrest."

"Zip it. Pro's should know the rules that

Sundays are taboo."

Paterson gets in the car. Gilmour drives the car off. Charlie shouts after them.

"Fascists!"

Dina, who has been watching from a distance, joins him.

"Fucking nicked them for nothing. That guy's a sadist. He'll beat them about the face so they can't work for a week.

"Where have they taken them?"

"To Pitt Street station."

Charlie thinks. He looks at Dina who is wearing a man's hat and long trench coat over her shoulders.

"Let me borrow your hat and coat, Dina."

There is such a look of determination in Charlie's face, Dina does as she is told.

"What are you going to do, man?"

"In the property business, everybody has a degree in law."

Charlie puts on the brimmed hat and trench coat. Dina looks down at Charlie's feet and the beat-up trainers.

"You're going to need some shoes."

Charlie nods. Dina smiles.

"I'll ask Foxy."

Nearby, there is a skip full of office rubbish. Charlie rakes in the skip. He pulls out a dusty old briefcase and dusts it down.

Gina is sitting alone in a Pitt Street station cell. She has been knocked about and her face is reddened, but no skin has been broken.

The cell door opens and a POLICEWOMAN enters.

"You're a lucky girl. Your solicitor's here. Follow me."

Gina is shown into the detention room where Lucy is already waiting. Charlie has his hat pulled over his face, but as Gina sits down, she sees that it is him.

"Charlie!"

"Shoosh! I'm Michael Stirling, your solicitor. Are you okay?"

"No. But not as bad as her. Look."

Gina urges Lucy to put her right foot up on the bench. Her toes are black and blue.

"Who did that!"

"Paterson tried to break my toes by stamping on them."

"I'll have you out of here in five minutes."

The DUTY SERGEANT is behind the front desk. Charlie addresses him in a high handed way.

"I want my clients released now, or I will file a complaint about police brutality."

"Your clients have been charged with soliciting."

"Sergeant, if you do not comply with my wishes, I will call for a police surgeon to examine them."

The Sergeant suddenly realises that he has a situation on his hands.

"It was Detective Constables Paterson and Gilmour who arrested your clients. Perhaps you should speak with them?"

"I'm not going to speak to thugs. I will only speak with the Chief Inspector, or I will go to the press."

The Sergeant is now deeply concerned.

"Take a seat please, sir."

In a back room, Paterson is sitting reading the Sunday Post. Gilmour is hovering over a filing cabinet.

The Duty Sergeant enters the room.

"Detective Constable Paterson!"

Paterson's face screws up. He and the Sergeant are old enemies.

"You're a psychopath, Paterson! I'm letting those girls go!"

"Fuck you, MacDonald!"

Gilmour shakes his head in disbelief at the exchange. MacDonald leaves the room and Paterson goes back to reading the cartoon section of his paper.

Charlie is waiting by the door on the other side of the partition as Gina and Lucy walk out free. The Sergeant pushes Gina and Lucy's belongings over the counter. Charlie appreciates the uniformed copper's fairness.

"Thank you, sergeant."

Gina is supporting Lucy who is limping heavily.

"Just keep them off the streets on Sundays."

Charlie nods.

Outside the police station, Gina and Lucy are grateful.

"Thanks. If we'd gone up in front of sheriff we'd have got three months."

"Not for a first offence?"

"I've been done before" Lucy admits.

"I've done thirty days for shop lifting." Gina adds. "I'm a known thief."

Gina and Lucy laugh. Charlie is not sure if they are serious or not.

"You mean I risked my neck for two jailbirds?"

Gina is quick to reject the idea that she is a villain.

"Heh, wait a minute. I've never done a trick in my life. I was fixed up there."

"Okay, I'm sorry."

Charlie takes the hat and trench coat off. He opens the briefcase, takes out his hobo coat, and throws the briefcase away.

"Look give this stuff back to Dina. Tell Foxy I'm keeping the shoes for the day."

He turns his back on them and starts to walk away.

"Where are you going?"

"I'm just going to hide away until Tuesday comes."

"But we had a date?"

"A date? Are you kidding me?"

Gina thrusts the hat and coat into Lucy's hands. She goes after him.

"You can't run out on me like that."

"Says who?"

"Says me."

Gina spins him around. Their eyes meet.

"We're still going for that swim."

"It's the afternoon. The weather's lousy."

"It's only a half hour train journey."

"What about Lucy?"

Lucy has caught up with them.

"I can look after myself."

Charlie gives in. Gina gives a little flickering smile of delight. She takes Charlie's hand. He pulls his hand away in embarrassment. Gina gives a little laugh and skips on ahead. She turns and shouts back to Lucy.

"See you later, Luce."

Lucy half-smiles in self pity at being left behind. She watches them go.

On the station platform, Gina is reading the timetable. Charlie is standing looking at the sky.

"What happens if it rains?"

"We get wet. There's a train in two minutes."

"So we just get on without tickets?"

"No. We pay."

Gina pulls out a twenty pound note from the lining of her pants.

"Where did you get that?"

"It's what's left of my giro."

"You're up to all the tricks."

"You've just had an easy life."

"I've had my share of hard times."

"Like when?"

"Like when I first left Glasgow when I was fifteen."

"Fifteen?"

"I ran away to my brother's in London. He made me go back to school down there. I went on to do law at the LSE. It was the glorious Thatcher years."

"It was the Goody Snatch years."

"Maybe. Some good things came out of it, some bad things."

"Christ. How old are you? Fifty Get real."

The train carriage is quiet. Gina and Charlie share a forward facing seat. Gina is at the window.

"This is fun. I haven't taken a train for years."

"Why not?"

"I drive everywhere, even in London. I hate the tube."

Gina suddenly sees someone further down the carriage that she knows.

"Oh shit ..."

Gina immediately slides down the seat to make her self small.

"What's up?"

"It's Rab."

Gina's lanky looking ex-husband RAB is in his early twenties. He sits down on the seat opposite them.

"Hi, Georgina. Remember me?"

"How could I forget you, Rab."

"What you doing these days?"

Gina concocts a lie.

"I've remarried."

"Really ... so have I. I've got two kids. That's Karen."

Rab points to his young wife KAREN with their TWO YOUNG CHILDREN. he lowers his voice so Karen can't hear.

"Look, I'm sorry it didn't workout between us. It took me ages to find out that Kenny was a rat. He tried to do the same thing to Karen. In the end, I put him in hospital."

"That's nice. Just like me, then?"

Rab smiles awkwardly, seemingly lost for words.

"Is this your new shag then?"

Charlie is angered by Rab's attitude.

"I think you should go back to your new wife now, okay."

The train has stopped at a station and Karen is waiting to get off.

"Just trying to be civil. See you, Georgina."

Gina says nothing in reply. She is happy to see Rab leave the train. She is openly frustrated at not being able to leave the past behind.

Charlie takes her hand and gives it a squeeze. He looks at her feet resting on the seat opposite. Her toe nails are painted. He looks at her face.

"How's your face?"

"Nothing that a swim won't cure."

Lucy is walking along King Street with her head down thinking about her life. As she reaches the corner with Osborne Street, she looks up and her face fills with horror.

Paterson and Bingo Brown are arguing.

Lucy starts retracing her steps but is met by Tommy. Tommy grins. Lucy ties to go round him, but Tommy grabs her by the throat and yanks her off in the direction of Bingo who is shouting at Paterson.

"Yer're overstepping the line, copper. We hud an arrangement."

"If you don't up the kickbacks, then I'm going to call in all the warrants on your Runners."

"Yer're a greedy swine. Yer mate Houston knew the limits."

"Houston's old news. Now you've got to me to deal with. Pay up, bozo."

Bingo hands over a fat envelop.

Tommy arrives with Lucy who is wide-eyed and terrified.

"Well, if it isn't your little runaway slave, Bingo."

"I'm nobody's slave. I hate you all!"

Bingo is hurt by Lucy's outburst.

"Let her gaw, Tommy. "

Paterson disagrees. "I don't think that's wise, Bingo. She knows what's going down."

"Ah said let her gaw."

Lucy is released and scurries away.

Paterson shakes his head.

"That girl's trouble. She knows enough to bring us all down."

"Ye lay wan finger oan her, and Ah'll kill ye, fucker."

Bingo is waving a finger in Paterson's face. Paterson smiles. They stare each other out.

"Now, now, Mister Brown, don't forget I'm the law."

Gina and Charlie have reached Loch Lomond and are walking on the sands by the loch-side. She is barefooted in the water. He is walking along the margin.

"It's not far. Just around the bend."

"You come out here a lot?"

"I haven't been here since I was a kid."

There is a splash of water and a scream. Gina is in the water. Charlie is half naked on the shore.

"Come on, old man! Get in before the midges get you!"

Charlie takes off the last of his clothes and half-runs, half-dives into the water. He screams with cold.

"Jesus Christ! My monkeys have dropped off."

They both laugh. Gina swims up to Charlie.

"I better help you search for them."

She kisses him.

Charlie goes to say something but Gina puts her hand over his mouth.

"Don't ....."

"Don't what?"

"Don't say anything stupid."

"But I want to say something stupid."

Gina kisses him again. Charlie responds with passion.

"Can you feel anything?"

"I'm so cold I can't feel a thing."

"Nor can I."

They both laugh, then instantly start making towards the shore.

Gina and Charlie are partially dressed and sitting on the beach. Gina is drying her hair with a towel she has pulled from her bag. Charlie has made a fire.

"Where did you learn to do that?"

"Boy's Brigade. I did a lot of camping."

Gina is amused by his past.

"You don't look the type."

"There's lots of us out there."

"Ex-boys' brigade?"

"No ... guys who don't look the type."

They kiss. Charlie's hand reaches to fondle her breasts.

Gina sinks with him backwards. Charlie is surprised by the heat of her passion as she slides the palm of her hand down into his forest of Eden. He gives to her.

"What about the midges?"

Gina whispers. "They can stay and watch."

It is two hours later. Gina and Charlie are walking hand in hand back towards the small town of Balloch.

"What do you really want to do with your life, Gina?"

"I missed out on going to college. I'd like a nice house. I'd like to have kids ... all the things that most people want."

"Caroline doesn't want kids."

"Why are you with her then?"

Gina and Charlie are sitting, on a park bench licking ice-cream cones, as they wait for the train back to Glasgow.

"I think Caroline and I have reached the end of the road. She's so materialistic ... everything has got to be just right for her, and nothing I ever seem to do is good enough."

"Do you love her?"

"Someone else asked me that the other day. Isn't that strange?"

"You still haven't answered my question?"

"I talk about her a lot. I care about what she thinks about me."

"Do you have separate bank accounts?"

"Of course we do."

"Then you're not in love."

"How can you say that?"

"I know. When you love someone, you share everything with them."

"Even your money?"

"Especially your money. It's always money that stands in the way of love."

Gina stands up. She reaches for her bag.

"It's time we were getting back.

"Let me carry your bag."

"Okay, but treat it with care. It was a birthday gift from my foster parents."

"I always treat other people's things with care."

"You better wipe that dog shit off Foxy's shoes then."

"What dog shit?"

Charlie inspects his shoes. He is disgusted.

"Aw, man. That's gross."

Charlie starts wiping his shoe on the grass. Gina laughs. Charlie wipes and hobbles and races to keep up with her.

"What's the matter with people letting their dogs shit anywhere like that ......"

Charlie catches up Gina just as two old ladies walking their dogs pass her on the path.

Hotshots, Quayside. Paterson, and his ex-partner NEIL HOUSTON are playing ten-pin bowls. Paterson has a deep rooted resentment towards Houston as he blames Houston for the breakdown of his marriage.

"I'm telling you, Neil. Gilmour is a snitch. No-one comes back from the Met still a DC."

"Just keep your nose clean, Col. I'll be out for a year, then they'll have to re-instate me for lack of evidence. Then we'll go back to the routine we know."

"The chief's noticed that all I seem to

pull in is fry. He wants a shark.

"Give him Brown."

"Are you serious? "

Paterson is cagey. Houston is equally cautious.

"I can't collect from Brown any more. You know that?"

Paterson nods. Houston hands out his advice

"If he's run in, he'll keep his mouth shut and do his time. Go for the dossers and paper sellers. They all owe Brown money. Burn out a few skippers and the message will go around that none of the scum are safe. Use the pretext that you're looking for runaways."

"How does that help us with Brown?"

Houston has an evil look in his eye.

"Scare the scum on the streets, and disrupt their incomes, and someone will turn in Brown before he has time to baseball them for the loans they can't repay. Let Gilmour take the credit. Got me?"

"Sure, Neil. But won't you still go down?"

"When the chips are down, the boys in blue stick by their own. How's your little girl?"

"She's going to America for the summer."

"Christ, isn't it great these days. We get to play skittles, and the kids get to go to America."

Bingo Brown is sitting in a car counting money. Tommy throws Snitch into the back of the car. Snitch's nose is bleeding.

"Whit's he got to say for himsel', Tommy?"

"He says the cops are out to get you, Bingo."

"Whit they wannt me fur, Snitch?"

"It's that Gilmour."

"The new cop oan the block?"

"He's efter Paterson's arse. Word's oot Paterson knows it and he's goan tae trade ye in tae keep his job."

"How'd ye know aw this, Snitch?"

Tommy stretches Snitch's neck and twists. Snitch squeals.

"Houston tolt me. He found oot that it wis Paterson who shopped him tae the cops. Noo he wants his payback. He says that Paterson has been making moves oan Lucy and thought ye should know."

"She hates the fucker. Who's she really seeing, Snitch?"

"Ah don't know, Bingo, ... honest."

"Ye tell everyone tae dae turkey fur a couple o' days. Okay?"

Bingo snaps his fingers and Tommy lets Snitch go. Snitch scurries out of the car. Tommy is worried.

"What are we going to do, Bingo?"

"We're goan tae think this over."

"Then what?"

"We're goan tae cripple Lucy's fancy man. Then, we're goan tae waste Paterson."

Lucy is back in her street clothes. She is trying to sell the Issue outside the Italian Centre on John Street. From the way she is propping herself up on a bollard, it is obvious she is taken some heroine. She is approached by JACK, the red-faced middle-aged, magazine street-supervisor.

"Alright, Jack?"

"I'm alright. Are you? Why are you no on your regular pitch? You know you can be arrested for selling on the wrong pitch."

"Give me a break, Jack. I've had a hard day. This is Foxy's pitch and he's away looking out for Dina."

Lucy's eyelids are drooping from taking her smack. Jack gives her a gentle shake.

"Aw, Lucy, darling why do you do it?"

"Can you not just leave me alone, Jack."

Jack is genuinely concern about her.

"Are you skippering at the moment?"

"Aye. I can't stand the hostels, they drive me crazy with their rules. I'm also not crazy about the clientele."

"I can never understand how a good looking lassie like you has ended up on the streets like this."

"Bad luck, Jack. I've never been very lucky. How come you've ended up a street supervisor?"

"I've never been lucky either."

They both laugh at each other's

misfortune.

"Can I ask you a question?"

"Go ahead."

"Just suppose a homeless girl like me met a handsome rich man, how would she get him to love her?"

"Like Cinderella you mean?"

"Sort of ... How would she cut through all that prince charming crap?"

"Men are men aren't they?" Jack is curious. "Have you found a Prince Charming?"

"With my luck? No chance .... I always seem to mess up...?"

Jack gives her a little friendly tap on the shoulder.

"Och, well, hen .... cheer up."

He turns and leaves Lucy propped against the bollard. Lucy is too absorbed in her one world to watch him go.

Gina and Charlie emerge from the High Street train station. The sun is just going down and their is a long shaft of sunlight striking along the old cobbled lane they are walking hand in hand in. Gina stops and leans against the lane wall. She pulls Charlie into her.

"What'd you want to do, now?"

Charlie wants to go with Gina wherever she is going but doesn't want to appear pushy.

"I should go back to the hostel for the night. It's better than the street? What about you?"

"I share a place with Lucy. She gets funny if I bring guys back with me ...."

"I wouldn't get in the way ... It's just, well, I look on you as the only friend I've got right now."

Gina blushes. She softens her resolve.

"Our place is a bit makeshift. I mean, it's not the sort of place you'll be used to ... being rich and that."

"Right now I'm just the same as you. In fact, I'm a whole lot poorer than you. You at least have a home."

"Well, as long as you don't think that I can't keep house. I'm very organised in my own way."

"I believe you."

"Come on, then. It's not far. In fact I think you'll recognise it as soon as you see it."

Chapter 4

The 'skipper' is in a corner of the wasteland that Charlie sold for a half million two days earlier. The 'skipper' is little more than a make-shift lean-to against an old brick wall. There are a few personal items that belong to Gina and Lucy but little else.

Lucy is sitting with Willie-Boy and Steamer. She is painting stones with water colours. Willie-Boy has found a music station on an old radio. They are drinking a bottle of vodka.

"What d'you think, doll? Mega trash, or what?"

Lucy is enjoying the music. Steamer is not.

"It's pish."

Willie-Boy dismisses Steamer's opinion.

"This is the latest, man. Ask the doll?"

Lucy mocks Willie-Boy. "It's better than you're singing"

Willie-Boy gives Steamer a big 'I told you so' grin.

Gina and Charlie arrive. Gina is not pleased at seeing the boys.

"This is our skipper ...."

"Give us a break, Gina. The cops are after us."

Steamer points to Charlie.

"It's his fault Smokey got nicked."

Willie-Boy nods in agreement.

"How's it my fault?"

Steamer is adamant. "You told us you were loaded."

"That's right, man" Willie-Boy adds. "We were trying to save you, man. Get your credit cards."

"You broke into the pound?"

Steamer throws in an observation.

"You should have seen the size of the dug."

Willie-Boy dents Steamer in the ribs with his elbow to shut him up.

"That's some car, man. I saw the dog coming at me in it. The gleam on it saved me six months in jail."

Gina is not impressed.

"You're a bunch of idiots."

"Smokey will tell the cops we were in on it ... that's why we can't go back to the hostel. Let us kip here, man?

Lucy jumps in on behalf of Willie-Boy.

"Let them stay, Gina. He's got vodka."

Willie-Boy's eyes light up

"And scran, man. We did some shopping at Tescos."

Willie-Boy and Steamer produce four plastic bags of food and drink which they have obviously stolen. Steamer forces a bottle of vodka on Charlie.
"Do you think you can forgive Willie-Boy for scratching you're paint work with his crowbar?"

"For fuck's sake, Steamer. You're always putting me in it." Willie-Boy pulls out a box of cracker bread.

"Anyone for crackers?"

Lucy is quick on the uptake.

"You're crackers."

They all laugh

They have made a blazing fire. The music is cranked right up. Willie-Boy and Gina are dancing. Steamer, well drunk, is lazing in front of the fire. Willie-Boy is in his element.

"This is brilliant, man. You've a great place here, doll."

Charlie and Lucy are lounging on some sleeping bags.

"How long have you been here, Lucy?"

"A couple of weeks. The last skippers got burnt out by the bizzies."

"What for?"

"You tell me. This is just a bit of wasteland. It's worth nothing."

Charlie goes to say something but says nothing. Steamer throws some large pieces of wood on to the fire. Lucy is annoyed.

"Quit it, Steamer! Someone'll call the fire brigade."

The dance song on the radio fizzles out. Gina and Willie-boy join Charlie and Lucy on the sleeping bags. Willie-Boy is in a jokey mood.

"Well, man, have you thought how you're going to get your car back yet?"

"Nope. Any ideas?"

"Why don't you mug an old lady when she comes out the post office with her pension."

Steamer thinks Willie-Boy is serious.

"You're a bastard, Willie."

"I'm only joking, Steamer."

Charlie and Willie-Boy are half-cut. Steamer has drunk to excess. He has passed out.

"Can you believe he's only twenty eight?"

"He looks about forty."

"That's the streets for you, man. I read in the Issue that people like him are dead by the time they're forty two. Isn't that right, Gina."

"People like you, Willie-Boy."

"No way, man. I'm going to cut down on the drugs. I'm going to live until I'm ninety."

Willie-Boy throws his arm around Lucy.

"In your dreams."

"You're in my dreams, doll."

Willie-Boy gives Lucy a kiss on the cheek. She is flattered, but pretends bravado.

"And you're my worst nightmare, you dope peddler."

Lucy takes in a mouthful of beer.

"Now is that a nice way to talk about your boyfriend?"

Lucy throws Charlie a look.

"He's been trying to get it up me for the last six months."

"I'm in love with you. Why don't you marry me and we'll settle down in a nice we cottage in the highlands."

"He's nuts. What would I want to live in the middle of nowhere for?"

"Because I see it in your eyes. Deep down you're a country girl at heart."

Lucy blushes, as if Willie-Boy has struck a chord in her that has been lost.

"Och, Willie-Boy ... I'm a fuck-up."

Lucy draws away from the fire and hides herself in some blankets. Willie-Boy is self-doubting.

"I was just trying to cheer her up."
Gina gets up and goes to Lucy. She takes a vodka bottle with her. Charlie is left with Willie-Boy

"Have you got a beer there?"

Willie-Boy rustles in a Tesco bag and brings out a can of McEwan's lager. Charlie unzips it.

"What are you going to do? This life isn't for the likes of you?"

"It has it's appeal. It's the first time in my life I've been with a bunch of people I actually like."

"You're kidding me, man. We're a bunch of reprobates. We'd steal the shirt off your back."

"But you help each other out."

"Sure. This is great, man ... no responsibilities, good crack, but the downside is shit, man ..... The cops. The dealers. The lenders."

Willie-Boy takes a long drink. His tone changes.

"I owe two hundred quid. Tomorrow that goes up to four hundred. The original debt was twenty notes for two E's, but I missed making the payment, and it's been doubling ever since."

"We're both in the shit then."

"If don't go out and steal something tomorrow and hawk it for at least a hundred nicker, I can say goodbye to my legs."

"Why don't you just leave town?"

"Like you, man? There's things keeping me here. I've either got to square it with the lenders or I'm as good as a cripple."

"Can't the cops do something about it?"

"The cops are in on it, man. The dealers and lenders cut them in. Ask Gina. "

Gina has not been listening. He's out of it on vodka.

"Ask me what?"

"How to clear up this whole goddam mess the world's in?"

"Lock up the cops, shoot dealers, and cut off all moneylenders balls." She is angry. "People are making money out of us, but we're still being treated like garbage. We're human beings and look at the way we live! "

Willie-Boy throws in his two pence. "People hate us."

Gina is reflective.

"What have we ever done for them to despise us so much?"

Charlie thinks he's got the answer.

"I don't think the homeless are despised. I think they're pitied.

Gina blows up at Charlie.

"Screw them! We're human beings and this is our planet too. Look at us! Pushed onto a piece of wasteland like derelicts."

Willie-Boy nudges Charlie.

"You better calm her down, man. It's the drink."

"Piss off, Willie! It's not the drink, it's the truth! Do you think I like seeing my friends die in this miserable wasteland of a world? Drugs are blamed for all the world's problems. It's people's attitudes that kill. The cops! The politicians! The stinking social workers! The Millennium? The new Dark Ages is what we're entering! No-one gives a damn what happens to us!"

Charlie and Willie-Boy are trying to get Gina to sit down. Gina starts to lash out and socks Willie-Boy in the jaw. He goes down instantly. Gina sobers up a little.

"Willie-Boy? Did I do that? I'm sorry. It's the vodka."

"I think you should lie down."

Charlie gets Gina to sit down with him. She suddenly clings on to him.

"You're not leaving me, are you? You wouldn't leave me?"

"No, I'm not leaving .....

Willie-Boy groans.

"Some party, man."

Willie-Boy curls up to go to sleep.

Charlie strokes Gina's hair as she rest in his arms.

It is near dawn and the birds are singing. Charlie is awoken by the sound of car doors closing and the appearance of flashlights on the wasteland.

Charlie stirs Gina.

"Gina ... wake up."

It is Paterson, followed by Gilmour.

"Try over there ... by the wall."

Gina is wide awake. Experience has taught her to react.

"Lucy! Get up it's the bizzies!"

Charlie stirs Willie-Boy.

"The cops!"

Gina and Lucy gather together their belongings.

Willie-Boy clears off on his own.

Gina, Lucy and Charlie run off together.

Paterson appears at the skipper. He is carrying a plastic petrol can.

"Over here! "

Gilmour arrives with his flashlight. It is blinking on and off. Paterson is off-hand with him.

"Go after them! Go on! Go after them!"

Gilmour sees Willie-Boy and chases after him.

Paterson unscrews the cap on the petrol can.

Gina, Lucy and Charlie have reached the edge of the wasteland. Lucy suddenly turns back.

"Lucy!"

"I've dropped my giro book. Wait for me."

Lucy starts to run back towards the skipper.

Paterson is pouring the petrol over Steamer and kicking him with his foot.

"Get up you scumbag."

Steamer is groaning in a half conscious way.

Paterson takes out his lighter and ignites it.

"Get up, bampot."

He holds a petrol soaked rag in one hand and his lighter in the other

Lucy returns to the edge of the skipper. She looks around the wall. She sees Paterson standing over Steamer with the lit rag.

Paterson tosses the rag on to Steamer's petrol soaked sleeping bag.

Lucy lets out a scream.

Paterson turns and recognises her.

Lucy turns and runs.

There is a backdraft from the flames which prevents Paterson from chasing after her.

Lucy runs into Gilmour who grabs hold of her arm.

Their eyes meet.

Gilmour, with a flick of his eyes, lets go of her arm.

Lucy runs.

Gina and Charlie are anxiously waiting at the perimeter of the wasteland. Lucy appears.

"Paterson has torched Steamer. He's set him on fire!"

Gina is shocked.

"Oh my god ....."

Charlie is suddenly enraged. He makes to go back into the wasteland but Gina holds him back.

"Don't!"

Lucy has broken down into hysterics.

"He saw me see him do it!"

"I'm not putting up with this shit any more! It's murder! We're going to the police!"

Lucy panics and pleads with Charlie.

"Please! I'll never live long enough to be a witness.

"For god's sake, what are you talking about! He's set fire to someone!"

Gina pulls Charlie's sleeve.

"He's a cop! Don't you understand that Lucy's life is in danger now."

"I can't accept this. This is no way for human beings to live!"

Gina snaps. Her thoughts are for Lucy's safety.

"Beat it, then! I'm not having you put Lucy's life at risk. Go on, piss off!"

"Suit yourself! I've had it with you people!"

Charlie walks away.

Gina cradles Lucy in her arms.

"Let him go back to London!"

Charlie keeps walking.

Gina continues to comfort Lucy.

Charlie is hanging on the end of a payphone.

"Yes, operator. Keep ringing."

Charlie looks out on to the city which is just starting to wake up.

"Caroline! Jesus, Caroline, you don't know how glad I am to hear your voice."

An ambulance goes by.

In London, Caroline is in her dressing gown. David is still with her. She is cranky.

"You've got a nerve calling me at this time in the morning."

"Caroline, I'm in trouble."

"Don't give me your excuses, Charles. Tell me straight. Are you're having an affair with someone."

"Caroline ... listen to me ..."

"You're still in Glasgow aren't you. There's only one thing that can be keeping you there and that's another woman."

"My car's in the pound ...."

"Answer me, Charles. Have you slept with someone else?"

Charlie bites his lip. He wants to lie but he can't bring himself to do it.

"It's not like you think ..... Caroline?"

Caroline slams down the phone.

In the phone-booth on a cold May morning, Charlie realises he has blown his one chance of rescue from the nightmare his weekend has become. He slowly hangs the receiver up and rests his head against the phone set. He hears the sound of the ambulance siren receding.

He looks up.

All traces of indecision drain from his face as he realises what he must do.

Gina and Lucy are sitting in the casualty ward waiting to hear news about Steamer's condition.

Charlie enters the ward and sees them both sitting. He quietly sits down beside them.

Each of them sit in their own world without saying a word.

Paterson and Gilmour emerge from a side entrance of the Royal Infirmary Hospital.

"This is bad, Paterson. You knew that geezer was there."

"I swear I didn't."

"I'm going to report you for this."

"We were searching for runaways. Instead we found one lousy scumbag. He didn't even have ID"

"We've got a name. That's what matters."

"You won't pin this one on me, pal."

"We'll see."

"I'm telling you. The report will go in and no-one will give a damn about a dosser. That's the way it is. The sooner you learn about how we do things in Glasgow, the sooner you'll get out my face."

"You don't belong in a modern police force. Your kind of policing is only practised in places like Serbia."

"Don't shed tears for the scum, Gilmour. Maybe you should be working for Amnesty International."

Back in the casualty ward, a NURSE comes through a swing door. She approaches Charlie and the two girls and shakes her head.

Lucy jumps up and rushes out crying.

Gina puts her head in her hands.

Charlie gets up and kicks a chair. The Nurse tries to calm him. She gets Charlie to sit back down and put his arm around Gina. She throws his arm off as if to say it is all his fault. Gina grabs her jacket and rushes out.

Charlie is dejected.

Gina emerges from the hospital. Lucy is dejectedly leaning against a wall. She wears her life on her face and it looks empty.

Gina takes her arm and they move off. Charlie emerges from the hospital and follows sheepishly behind.

Down on Argyll Street, Willie-Boy is eyeing up a shop window with the intention of doing a quick smash and grab.

A hand taps him on his shoulder. He turns.

Tommy, Gerry and Ann-Marie are towering over him. Tommy grins.

"You owe us some money, pal."

"Give us another few hours, Tommy."

Ann-Marie pushes a baseball bat into Willie-Boy's ribs.

"Sorry, mate, you've defaulted on the terms. You're bankrupt."

"Please, Tommy, can you give me time to asset strip?"

"No chance. Bingo's called in the liquidators."

Gerry and Ann-Marie are dragging Willie-Boy down an alley. Tommy pulls out the baseball bat from up his sleeve. At the sight of the bat Willie-Boy starts to sweat.

"Will you go easy, Tommy. I've just asked a lassie to marry me."

Gerry and Ann-Marie pin Willie-Boy against a doorway. Tommy swings the bat down on to one of Willie's knees. There is a loud crack and a howl of pain from Willie. He almost passes out. Gerry and Ann-Marie keep him pinned to the door.

The bat comes down again on Willie's other knee. The pain makes Willie-Boy pass out. Gerry and Ann-Marie let Willie fall into the gutter.

Gina and Lucy have been followed into nearby Glasgow Cathedral by Charlie. Gina and Lucy are sitting on wicket chairs placed against a stone column. Charlie is pacing up and down.

"Look, why are you still hanging about with us?"

"I want to help."

"You're the one that needs the help. You're dragging us down."

"I feel so useless."

"Why don't go and see your parents. They'll give you the money to get your car back. Then we'll see the back of you."

"I left on bad terms with my parents."

"Look, we all left on bad terms with our parents. That doesn't stop us from seeing them from time to time."

"I can't."

"You're so full of shit. Look at the state of you."

"Christ! What do you expect? I've just slept out in a rubbish heap overnight. I'm used to sleeping at the Hilton."

Lucy is annoyed.

"That was our home."

"Home? Who are you kidding! Bloody cave men lived better than you two do. I'm off to pray for you! At least I'll be warm."

Charlie walks off towards the cathedral altar.

Gina remains staring at her feet. Lucy thinks Gina is making a mistake.

"Go after him ...."

"No way. He's a dickhead."

"That's not true. Go after him."

"I don't need someone like him telling

me how to live my life."

"Yes you do. Go on. I'll be fine. I'll see if I can find Willie-Boy."

Gina is suddenly suspicious.

"What for?"

"To tell him about Steamer."

"Be careful, Luce ...."

Gina gives Lucy a long hug.

Lucy gets up and heads for the exit. Gina pauses for a moment to prepare herself, then enters further into the cathedral to find Charlie.

Charlie is looking at the roof as Gina approaches.

"It's amazing that it's been here for nearly fifteen hundred years."

Gina stares at the roof.

"Do you think we'll last more than two days?"

"Not without a Reformation."

Gina knows she's been too hard on Charlie.

"Can we make up?"

"I hope so."

Gina takes a little step forward and walks into Charlie's arms. Either of them are religious. They kiss, and keep on kissing for a long time.

Lucy is walking along the street quickly. She is apprehensive and alert. She has the sweats. She doesn't know where she will find Willie-Boy, or whether he can get her a fix.

Gina and Charlie are outside in the cathedral grounds. Charlie feels a cold shudder down his back and is suddenly worried about Lucy.

"Is Lucy okay?"

"I hope so. I never know what she's going to do next."

"You seem close to her?"

"People get close quickly when they are flung together. London was like that."

"You lived in London?"

"For awhile. It's not a place I can blossom."

"Where could you blossom?"

"Paris, Rome ... I like beautiful buildings."

"Maybe we should run off to Rome."

"You could sell beautiful buildings and I could do charity work with the sick and homeless."

"Sounds too p.c."

They both laugh loudly and make back towards the High Street.

Paterson is tailing Lucy in an unmarked car. He is driving with a pair of leather gloves on. Gilmour is staring ahead oblivious that Lucy is walking briskly along the pavement a hundred yards ahead.

Paterson pulls up the car. Gilmour looks at him.

"Meet me at Buchanan and George in fifteen minutes."

"Look, Paterson, I'm sick of your

walkabouts."

"I need to go to the bank! Okay? Just do it."

Paterson gets out of the car.

Lucy is now in a busier section of the town off Argyll Street. She is less conscious of being spotted and has her head down. She runs into Tommy talking to Bingo.

Bingo puts his arms around Lucy and squeezes her cheek. Tommy leers.

"Looking for your fancy man, darling?"

"Not now, Bingo."

"You'll come back to me."

"Forget it, you psychopath. I'm never coming back to you. I've found someone else."

"He'll not be taking you dancing, that's for sure."

Hatred darkens Lucy's face. She immediate guesses.

"What have you done?"

"He's been discharged. If he behaves himself he can start trading again in three years time."

Bingo lets Lucy go. She runs off.

Bingo and Tommy laugh.

Lucy finds Willie-Boy in the alley. He has managed to drag himself up against a wall.

"I never knew this lane was so good for ham and egging."

"Aw, Willie. Can you get up?"

"Sorry, doll. I might have to take up residence here."

"I'll call an ambulance."

Lucy starts up the alley. Near the top of the alley she is pulled into a cul de sac by Paterson. With his gloved hand over her mouth he drags her behind a dumpster.

"You saw me, you little tart? Didn't you? You saw me roast that scumbag?"

Lucy's eyes are full of fear. She starts to struggle and kick. She tries to dig her nails into Paterson's face.

"Fuck you!"

Paterson starts to squeeze Lucy's neck. Her face starts to go red. She struggles and kicks.

"You're just another statistic."

Paterson has her raised off the ground.

Her feet kick.

"Just another body in a skip."

Lucy's feet go lifeless. Paterson slackens his grip.

"Ease does it, sweetheart."

Paterson slips Lucy's body into the dumpster. He removes his gloves and puts them in his jacket pocket. He emerges back out into the alley. He sees Willie-Boy's legs sticking out into the alleyway.

"Fucking tramps everywhere."

Paterson walks towards Willie-Boy.

Willie Boy, now conscious, recognises Paterson. He covers his face, and pretends to be asleep.

Paterson kicks Willie-Boy's legs. Willie-

Boy groans in pain. Paterson takes his gloves out and forces them onto Willie-Boy's hands.

"Another open and shut case."

Paterson walks on and leaves by the far side of the alley.

Willie-Boy has found himself a skateboard and is dragging himself along on top of it like a Calcutta beggar. His legs are drenched in blood.

A shadow falls over him.

"Fuck sake, Willie-Boy."

It is Snitch. "Lucy went for an ambulance but she never showed."

Willie-Boy pulls the gloves out of his pocket.

"Then that bent copper came down the alley. I pretended I was out of it. He stuck these on my hands. I thought I better drag myself out of there as quick as I could."

Willie Boy is in obvious pain.

"You couldn't get me to hospital could you. I'd like to keep my legs.

"Sure, Willie-Boy."

Snitch takes the gloves and puts them in his own pocket.

Gina and Charlie are crossing Albion Street. A NEWS-SELLER is selling the early edition of the Evening Times. His news box reads 'City Centre Body Found'. Gina's face goes gunshot white.

"What's the matter?"

"It's Lucy. I know it's Lucy."

Gina rummages for some change and buys a paper. She stares numbly at the paper. Her hands are shaking. She turns to Charlie.

"What are we going to do?"

Charlie puts his arm around her.

"Nothing until we are sure."

The soup-kitchen. Gina, Charlie, Dina, Betty, Foxy, and Snitch are all huddled around a table. They are all staring at the gloves which Snitch has produced.

"That's Paterson's gloves fur sure."

Dina shakes her head in disbelief.

"This is bad crack, man."

"Bingo'll go crazy when he finds oot. He's a very moral guy." Snitch adds.

Dina looks at Snitch. "Bingo Brown? You're joking."

"He wis soft oan her."

"We were all soft on Lucy, Snitch."

Gina is close to tears. Charlie decides to take charge.

"How much does it cost to hire a hit man?"

"Are you serious, man?" Dina reacts.

"This guy has killed two of us."

Gina looks at Charlie, proud that he considers himself one of them. However, her eyes betray that she is worried about Charlie's intentions.

Foxy scratches his head.

"How much would it cost to do a copper, Silky? Two thousand?"

"Five, Foxy."

Charlie is listening and thinking.

"I can get you the money."

"Charlie ....." Gina pleads.

"I've a ten thousand limit on my credit cards."

Gina is close to tears.

"But you haven't got your credit cards. They're locked up in your car."

"That's right. All I need is the fine, plus three days at twelve a day ... that's one hundred and forty one pounds."

"God, we're lucky if we have fifty quid between us."

Dina gives Charlie a look of 'get real'. The others nod. Betty is suspicious.

"How do we know you're on the level?"

"Yeah" answers Foxy "You might just eff off."

"No way!"

Charlie is angry at his motives being called into question.

Gina tries to reason with him.

"You can't get your car out until tomorrow anyway."

"I know ..... Come on, guys, have faith."

"I don't know, man, maybe he didn't do it."

"He did it, Dina. We all know he did it."

They all nod their heads.

"Anyway, think about it, okay?"

Everyone hangs their heads.

Chapter 5

The weather has turned nasty. The rain is lashing down on Gina and Charlie who are now out on St.Vincent Street.

"They're frightened, Charlie."

"I know. I guess murder doesn't come easy to anybody who's basically decent."

"I know we've got to get the bastard, for Steamer's sake as well as Luce's ... but paying for him to be killed is not the way."

Charlie is hesitant. Gina senses his uneasiness.

"You're not going to run out on me again, are you?"

"I've still got unfinished business in London."

"That's more important than this?"

"It's just as important to me!"

Gina is disgusted by Charlie's behaviour.

"I don't understand you? I shouldn't have taken you swimming."

"You've got me all wrong. Caroline and I are over, but I've got to tell her."

Gina pulls out a phone card and thrusts it into his hand.

"Go and tell her, then!"

"You're a pushy bitch sometimes."

Gina shakes her head. She's sick of his put-downs.

"I'm going to the pictures. I'll be in the front row. If you don't show up, I'll know I was deluding myself all along." Gina pushes him out of the way. "Besides, I'm sure your *woman* can charge a room at the Hilton for you!"

Gina hurries away into the rain.

Charlie lingers, looking at the phone-card, before pushing it into his jacket pocket and going off in search of the nearest call box.

The eighth floor in a busy London office shared by a number of businesses. Caroline is sitting at her office desk. David is at a desk opposite.

Caroline is on the phone. It's Charlie.

"You've a nerve."

"I need you to send me some money."

Caroline looks across to David to see if he can hear what is being said by Charlie.

"You've a cheque for half a million pounds, for god's sake."

"It's a bank holiday here."

Caroline is not amused.

"Is this one of your jokes, Charles? Do you want our partnership to fold?"

"To tell you the truth, I don't give a damn any more."

"Need I remind you that you only own twenty percent of this business?"

David has picked up the other line to listen in.

"Fine you can have it! And keep the house! I've had it with being a slave to money."

Caroline and David exchange glances.

"You'll not be saying that when you

are penniless."

"Piss off! "

"You're a fool, Charles. I'll shut all the doors I've opened for you."

"London's not the only city in the world."

"Where would you go ... Leeds, Liverpool, Dundee? "

"Rome!"

Caroline is completely thrown by Charlie's reply.

"And tell David I know he's been fucking you for months."

Caroline slams down the phone.

The Odeon Cinema, Renfield Street. Gina is in the front row of an almost empty theatre watching a contemporary low-life Scottish film called *The Ratcatcher*.

She is crying for Lucy.

Charlie appears and sits down beside her and puts his arm around her. She buries her head in his shoulder.

"Well, the business in London is all sorted out."

"So you'll be sleeping in the Hilton tonight?"

"Those days are over."

"I wouldn't mind spending a night in the Hilton."

"There's much better hotels."

Gina smiles.

"Look, if I went to see my parents, I'm sure they'd give me the cash to get my car back."

"What happened between you?"

"My mum remarried when I was fourteen. I didn't like my step-dad. One night I came in drunk. We had a big fight. I hit him with a chair, and I ran like hell.

"And you never went back?"
"What for?"
"To see your mother?"
Charlie thinks deeply about this.
"Now's your chance ...."
"They live on the Southside."
"That's not so far ......"

A quiet tree-lined street on the Southside of the city. Charlie and Gina stand facing an pre-WWII council house. It is old and dilapidated.

Seeing the house after fifteen years presents Charlie with a flush of childhood memories. Gina squeezes his hand. Charlie takes a deep breath and leads Gina through the garden gate.

Charlie rattles the letter-box. There is a long empty silence. It seems like ages before the door is finally opened by a grey-haired sixty-five year old woman.

It is CHARLIE'S MUM. She is speechless.

Charlie is equally speechless at seeing his mother after so many years.

Charlie's Mum starts to cry and throws her arms around Charlie's neck. Gina stands watching.

Charlie reaches out and takes Gina's

hand, and they all go inside.

It is morning and Charlie's Mum removes an orange earthenware jar from a shelf. She opens it and begins to count out one hundred and forty-one pounds in fivers and single Scottish pound notes.

Charlie and Gina emerge from the house. Charlie is freshly dressed and has a look of determination and purpose.

There is a taxi waiting.

Charlie is handed a small brown envelop by his mother. Charlie hugs her. His step-father appears behind her. Charlie shakes his hand. Gina is hugged by them both.

Charlie and Gina get in the taxi. It is an emotional parting for them all, for they still cannot find the words to bridge the fifteen estranged years. Charlie clutches the brown envelope. His whole life goes through his mind. He looks back through the taxi window.

His parents are waving.

Charlie waves back, then turns and emits a warm smile of satisfaction that he has bridged his past. Gina kisses him.

Gina and Charlie have returned to the wasteland and the burnt-out skipper which is a charred remain. Gina goes to a crevice in a brick wall and produces a smoke charred signing-on book. She gives it a wipe.

"Lucy's ......"

Gina makes a small cairn of painted stones in honour of Lucy. She places a small bunch of wild flowers on the cairn.

Charlie stands just behind her.

"I don't know what I would have done without you."

"You would have stayed at the Hilton."

Charlie puts his arms around Gina.

"I'll be back for you."

"Sure ..... And I'll be here."

"I mean it."

"That'll make it three days."

Charlie kisses her, then turns and goes.

At the city pound, Charlie puts the cash down on the counter. The Clerk takes the money and gives him a brief glance.

"I hope you enjoyed your holiday."

Charlie face relives the previous three days, but he says nothing. The Clerk hands Charlie a receipt and presses a buzzer which opens a door to the pound lot.

Charlie finds his car. He reaches under the front chassis and produces a spare ignition key which has been taped to the underside. He goes to the boot, and presses the automatic pad on the key to release the lock. He notices the scratches of Willie-Boy's crowbar and shakes his head.

"Nutter ......"

He opens the trunk, takes his suit

jacket and puts it on. He opens his briefcase. He puts on his gold watch. He places his credit cards in his jacket pocket. He puts on some shades. He combs back his hair. He slams down the boot cover.

Charlie pulls up in the Porsche outside the Blythswood Square Nat West bank. He goes in carrying his briefcase.

Some minutes later, Charlie comes out of the bank. He gets back into the car.

Snitch is shuffling along the side of the square. Charlie sees him and pulls up his car.

"Snitch! Get in!"

Snitch does a double take. He can't believe his eyes.

He gets in the car.

"Ah can't believe this, man. It's unreal."

"It's real."

Charlie puts his foot hard to the throttle.

"Does Bingo know Paterson killed Lucy?"

"He's crazy, man. If he knew, he'd waste Paterson himsel'."

Charlie throws five thousand pounds on to Snitch's lap.

"Would this be enough to get him to do it?"

Snitch hands the money back.

"Fuck, man. He disnae need yer blood money. Show 'im the gloves."

"Where can we find Bingo?"
"Collecting the Monday books."

Bingo, Tommy and some of the Runners
are outside the Social Security office
accepting giro's as payment of
outstanding debts. They are operating
from a van. Bingo is wearing Charlie's
bomber jacket. He is reading about the
murder.

Snitch appears.

"Bingo! Ah've someone to show ye!"

Snitch shows Bingo the gloves. Bingo's
eyes light up.

"Paterson murdered Lucy. He did it."

Bingo does not need to be pressed. He
snatches the gloves.

"Close shop, Tommy ....."

Gilmour has driven the unmarked car up
and onto the wasteland. He and Paterson
are out of the car arguing.

"It's up, Paterson. Today's your last
day as a cop."

"You never fooled me, Gilmour. I knew
you were the Chief Constable's snitch the
day I saw you."

"You deserve everything that's going to
happen to you. You murdered that girl,
and I'm going to be the Crown's star
witness."

"You've got nothing, Gilmour."

"No? The shake-down of that girl? The
toe-breaking? The tailing of her ten
minutes before she died? You're dead for

thirty years."

Charlie is with Bingo and Snitch in his car. There is a baseball bat between Bingo's legs. They are watching Paterson and Gilmour argue.

Bingo's boys are in the van parked behind Charlie's car.

Bingo puts a hood over his head. He starts out of the car. Charlie sees his jacket.

"You should leave your jacket. It might be recognised."

Bingo nods. He takes the jacket off and throws it into the car. Charlie smiles to Snitch. It is time to leave.

They drive off.

Paterson has Gilmour up against the side of the unmarked car.

"You don't scare me, scumbag. What's stopping me wasting you?"

"You haven't got the guts. You only pick on helpless people."

"Fuck you!"

Paterson punches Gilmour in the belly and he doubles. He is about to hit him again, but he is grabbed from behind by three hooded Runners. Two other Runners grab Gilmour and throw a hood over his head and tie it. Paterson is being dragged further into the wasteland scrub.

Gilmour's wrists are bound from behind. He is thrown into the trunk of the unmarked car.

Paterson is dumped on the ground and is being kicked. He is surrounded by Bingo, Tommy, and two of the Runners - Gerry and Ann Marie. Bingo removes his mask.

"Bingo ... what's this all about?"

Paterson is already a mess from being kicked.

Bingo throws the gloves in Paterson's face. Paterson breaks into a smile.

"Ain't love a bitch."

Bingo whacks Paterson across the face with the baseball bat and again. Bingo hits him another four times on the head. Paterson squeals with pain then falls silent.

Tommy looks away.

The car is driven into the centre of the wasteland. Gilmour is hauled out of the trunk and thrown on the ground. Paterson is dumped in the trunk and it is closed. Two of the Runners pour petrol in the windows of the car. Bingo signals everyone but Tommy to leave. They obey. Tommy hands Bingo a lighter. Gilmour groans on the ground.

"Don't kill me ... Please."

Bingo indicates Tommy to drag Gilmour away from the car. Tommy obeys. Bingo lights some rolled up sheets of paper and tosses the lighted sheets into the car.

There is an instant ball of flame.

Bingo smiles. He turns to walk away, but without warning the car explodes. Bingo is thrown forward by a sheet of flame.

A billow of smoke rises upward.

Bingo lies sprawled on the ground. Tommy tries to get Bingo up, but the sound of a police car siren makes him take to his heels.

Gilmour lies wriggling on the ground, crying.

Gina is out selling the Issue on Royal Exchange Square. She is not her usual outgoing self, and is standing half-dazed as the world passes her by.

Charlie's car suddenly pulls up in front of her on the pavement. Charlie leans over and opens the passenger door. Snitch gets out.

Gina is in an open-mouthed state of shock. The magazines drop from her hands.

"I told you I'd be back."

Gina hesitates for a split moment, then grabs her bag and throws herself into the car."

Gina is still slightly dazed. Charlie hands her the bomber jacket.

"Present for you ...."

Gina kisses him on the cheek.

Charlie puts the car into gear.

Snitch stands and watches then go.

The car is now on the motorway. Gina has her jacket on and the top is down. Her hair is streaming in the wind. Charlie is upbeat.

"Fancy some pizza?"

Gina looks at him as if he's crazy. He hands her the five thousand pounds.

"We'll have to find a place to live in Rome?"

Gina is reassured that they have a future together. She relaxes and decides to contribute to their future plans.

"We'll just have to find a skipper of our own."

Charlie pushes out into the fast lane and speeds his cool yellow Porsche southwards towards Carlisle.

ROBBIE MOFFAT

The author was born and schooled in Glasgow. He took a degree in English language and Literature at Newcastle University. He began writing when he was seventeen and has a had a career as a poet, novelist, playwright and screenwriter. He is best known for his feature film work in which he is also a director and producer.

His prose writing as been overshadowed by this. He wrote his first novel when he was twenty two and continued to write novels for the next twenty years. None of them were published.

The rediscovery of his prose work has lead to a recent spate of publications that has lead to a resurgence of interest in his prose writing.

www.ingramcontent.com/pod-product-compliance
Lightning Source LLC
Chambersburg PA
CBHW070504130626
46555CB00003B/1144